A Dark White Postscript

by

E. R. Bills

2023

STARKWEATHER IMPRINTS

PRAISE FOR E. R. BILLS'S WRITING

A "standout" story. "An elderly man is found burned to ash in his East Texas home, with no damage done to the floor or furniture, and when the local sheriff looks into his town's history of racial violence, the story mines Texas' own to haunting, sad effect."
–FORT WORTH WEEKLY

E.R. Bills writes in a straightforward, linear fashion presented mostly in chronological order, but the tales he presents are fascinating and perfect for campfire storytelling. Ever wondered about those abandoned small homes on the side of the highway hollowed out and overgrown with wild vines? How about those once prosperous places turned ghost towns where the wind whistles through the broken windows and windmills hauntingly creak in the silence? Bills brings those places to life . . . Gripping stories fill these pages.
–FORT WORTH MAGAZINE

Bills's writing harkens back to an earlier, pulpier era of paperback true crime. His prose style is lean and matter-of-fact, though he knows how to give each narrative a satisfying shape. **–KIRKUS REVIEWS**

E.R. Bills delivers the unexpected twists and turns, horrific plausibility and nightmarish world-building horror fans crave. **–Bret McCormick**, horror author & indy filmmaker.

Fixed for a Barbecue

An October 16, 1902 *Southern Mercury* newspaper headline announcing preparations for burning a Black man named Jim Buchanan at the stake in Nacogdoches, Texas.

This is the barbecue we had last night
My picture is to the left with a cross over it
your sons Joe.

Comments from the back of a lynching post-card featuring the charred remains of a Black man named Will Stanley after his lynching in Temple, Texas on July 31, 1915.

Here are the barbecued Niggers!

The popular holler after whites from Paris, Texas burned the Arthur brothers at the stake and then dragged their charred remains behind a car through the African American section of the city.

Nigger for breakfast!

A repeated taunt emanating from the white men who drug a Black man named David Gregory behind their car through the African American neighborhood of Kountze, Texas before they burned him at the stake on December 7, 1933.

*Where to start is the problem, because nothing begins
when it begins and nothing's over when it's over . . .*

Margaret Atwood

The figure was as black as sackcloth and it moved awkwardly in the dark. Tieg Bertram smelled it before he saw it.

It had an odor, like it was badly burnt. The reek was almost overpowering; but it was also familiar. Something that Bertram remembered from his past.

The figure moved closer.

Bertram lifted himself up on his elbows and looked around. An elderly man, his eyesight was bad in daylight, even with glasses. But at night, without them, he might as well have been blind. He didn't notice that only the form's lidless eyes and the front teeth of its lipless mouth caught light. The rest of its body was dark and indiscernible. Bertram could hear it, though. Its rough hide cracked as it moved.

"Hello," Bertram said. "Hello? Who's there?"

As Bertram sat up and fumbled for his glasses, the creature stopped.

Bertram retrieved his glasses from the nightstand and placed them over the bridge of his nose, securing the temple arms over his ears. Then, he flipped on the bedside lamp.

When Bertram's bleary eyes finally adjusted to the light, they abruptly widened and his jaw dropped. Before him stood a dark, twisted figure, solid black. His mind had problems processing it.

The creature stood motionless.

Bertram pushed the sheets and comforter away, swung his legs off the bed and faced the dark form. Except for its eyes and teeth, the scorched figure was as black as the grave. And with no lips, its countenance was frozen in a hellish grin.

"Hello," Bertram repeated weakly. The creature remained mute.

In Bertram's mind's eye, he knew this spectre, this grim form in the shape of a man. Its blackened contour, which looked as if it had been hewn from coal, now glistened in places where secretions of pus, pink with blood, gathered at the cracks in its hide.

It was grotesque, but Bertram was not afraid. There was something recognizable about this figure.

Bertram's memory was dim, but his mind began reaching back, sifting through the sedimentary layers of a long life. The creature was a man, or it had been a man. Bertram was sure of that.

The shadow remained motionless, its hands at its sides. The pungent smell it arrived with lingered like gloom. Bertram continued to stare.

A speck of memory flickered in one of the far corners of his consciousness, an inkling at first, evolving slowly and quietly. He turned his head and saw his face in the mirror above a chest-of-drawers.

The reflection of Bertram in the mirror was young and lean. His eyes were bright and his face was handsome and angular. His glasses were gone. It occurred to him that he couldn't have looked like that when he was any older than a teenager—and then it came to him.

He stared away for a moment and then turned back to the silent apparition. He looked it up and down slowly and his bottom lip quivered.

"That's not possible," Bertram said, as he looked back at the mirror, the face there now his face, the face of an old man. "That's . . ."

Bertram's protestation trailed off. The apparition stood idle, an unstirring totem.

Bertram turned back to the figure and peered into its lidless eyes. They stared straight ahead, above him, beyond him, the orbs seemingly immobile. Bertram lowered his gaze to one of its legs, a thick vine of charred sinew. A tear ran down Bertram's left cheek. Then, he looked, again, at the creature's eyes.

"Petty," Bertram said. "Pettigrew Smith."

The apparition's eyeballs shifted then, directly observing Bertram for the first time. Its bloodshot orbs seemed the only thing alive against its blackened head and torso. The rest of its burned carcass remained motionless.

"Is it really you, Petty?"

Bertram knew the answer.

He removed his glasses and wiped his eyes. Then, before turning back to the creature, he sniffed and folded his glasses and placed them on the nightstand.

"Oh god, Petty. It wasn't. . ."

Bertram placed his hands on his knees and then clasped them and let them rest in his lap.

"I'm sorry, Petty."

The dark creature moved then, unsteadily stepping towards Bertram, but Bertram didn't flinch or cringe. He held out his hand. The creature came close and slowly lifted its rigid right arm.

"Sorry, Petty," Bertram repeated.

The apparition touched Bertram's white, wrinkly fingertips with the nubs of its shriveled, charcoal knuckles, and Bertram burst into blue flame. The blaze roared orange and then yellow as it encompassed Bertram's body immediately and en masse. Bertram grunted, but nothing more.

The dark apparition stood over Bertram as the flames raged. When the fire began to die down, the spectre turned and shuffled away.

Sheriff Dunphee got the call on the radio about seven o' clock the next morning, just as he was leaving his home in Harkin.

Edna Jenkins in Troup had phoned the sheriff's department and said something had happened to her granddad, Bertram. But she couldn't explain what. When the dispatch officer pressed her for details, she grew agitated.

A little strange, Dunphee thought. But he knew Edna was harmless and getting up there in years. Their families were both from Harkin and Dunphee had even met Bertram once or twice, in Daingerfield or Ore City, he couldn't remember. Bertram had known Dunphee's grandmother, but had left Harkin when he was a young man. Dunphee had wound up back in Harkin after college, and Edna had moved to Troup ages ago when she married.

Troup was just southeast of Tyler and not far out of Dunphee's way. When he traveled through the town he always drove by the Troup Boxing Gym. It had originally been named after at a 16-year-old African American boxing phenom named Byron Payton, but the novelty and memory had worn off. Sheriff Dunphee had boxed against Payton in the late 1970s and lost in a decision; but only, he suspected, because Payton had gone easy on him.

Most of Dunphee's family and friends had been at the fight and assured him he was cheated, but he knew better. There was a way things were where they lived, and Payton's success simply rubbed white folks the wrong way.

Payton had been the complete package, a knockout punch (with either hand), a devastating jab and uncanny fist and foot speed. In retrospect, Dunphee knew that he was lucky he had even made it out of the ring alive and fairly sure he couldn't have beaten

Payton even if there'd been an extra Billy Dunphee in the ring with him. Payton's talent and determination had been spectacular. Dunphee had just been a tough country boy who was pretty good at taking a punch.

Payton had won the Texas Golden Gloves State Championship twice and was on his way to making the U.S. Olympic team in 1980—the year Reagan boycotted the summer Olympics. But Payton never got the chance to experience that disappointment. He and twenty-one U. S. boxers, trainers and coaches had perished in a plane crash on the outskirts of Poland a few months prior.

As Sheriff Dunphee drove through Troup, he wondered at it all over again. You never forget the first time you get laid out in a fight—especially in front of a large group of spectators.

It was what came to be known as a bolo punch. A hook combined with an uppercut. It dropped Dunphee immediately. He didn't even see it coming.

Dunphee was a plodder. It didn't hurt him, but it surprised him. When the bell rang and he got back to his corner, his trainer asked him if he was okay.

Dunphee nodded.

"Kid Galivan," his trainer said. "Sugar Ray Leonard. Scrunch up. *Economize.* And make him reach."

Dunphee didn't find out who Kid Galivan was till later. But he obviously knew who Sugar Ray was. Payton was shifty, but not showy. He was quick and punched with precision. He pared several of Dunphee's jabs and punches. He changed his lead foot a time or two. And his ducks, paws and feints were practically dizzying.

Dunphee caught Payton once and made him stumble. It was a counterpunch after he slipped a lead right. The mostly white crowd roared, but Payton was all business. If he smiled, it was only with his eyes. He didn't lose his temper. He just kept coming. He worked Dunphee over pretty good.

But it made Dunphee feel good, too.

Strike and parry. Absorb a blow, backpedal, reengage. Counterpunch. Body work. Dish it out and take it. Look for an opening. There was almost a rhythm to it. It was a good, honest contest. Mano y mano. No head butts. No silly point taps or fouling in the clinches. No razzle-dazzle. Dunphee had done his best.

Payton's invincibility in the ring had meant nothing in the end. All that was left was a statue dedicated to him and the others in Colorado Springs and an on-again, off-again annual boxing tourney held in his name at the Troup Boxing Gym. Dunphee sat ringside every year it was held.

When Dunphee had heard the news of Payton's death on the AM radio in his beat-up, old pick-up truck in 1980, he hadn't believed it. It didn't seem possible.

Now, an officer of the law for over twenty years, he knew anything was possible and sometimes the worst things.

Dunphee realized that maybe the best thing he'd ever done, perhaps the closest he'd ever come to a brush with greatness, was the match he'd had with Byron Payton. And the fact that the young man was gone still haunted him.

The boxing gym was one of the only things of note left in Troup, but Troup was practically cosmopolitan compared to Harkin. Harkin had showed some life early in the 20th century, but it sputtered out in the mid-thirties. Harkin barely had a post office. Tyler was beginning to expand out past them both, and Dunphee was thinking about moving away when he retired.

The Jenkins place was on a couple dozen acres just off State Highway 135 heading to Arp. When Sheriff Dunphee turned off on the gravel drive and crossed the cattleguard, he drove slowly so as not to disturb the handful of cattle and two nags that had run of the pasture. He parked under one of the big oak trees that sat out in front of the house, and Edna immediately appeared on the porch. She was nervous and fearful. Dunphee stepped out of the patrol car and took off his hat.

"Are you okay, Edna?" he asked.

"I don't know, Billy—*Sheriff Dunphee.*"

"You can call me Billy, Edna. You know that."

"Billy—I don't know what happened. I'm not sure what I'm seeing. I went in the spare bedroom I keep for my granddaughter when she visits, and he was—." Edna cupped a hand over her mouth and started to cry. Dunphee placed his hand on her shoulder and gave her a moment.

"Show me," he said.

Dunphee followed Edna into the house and recoiled when the stench hit his nostrils.

"It's bad, I know," Edna said. "But I didn't want to touch anything."

Dunphee put his hat back on and they took a left down a hall. Edna stopped at the last door on the right and held the doorknob. There was a towel at the base of the door, tucked there in an attempt to contain the odor.

"He's in here," Edna said. "I think. I didn't touch anything. I think it's him."

Edna opened the door and led Dunphee in. The smell got worse.

Noting the odor when he stood in Edna's entry, Dunphee had prepared himself for a spoiled cadaver, but there wasn't one. There was just a large pile of black and gray ash on the near side of the sheets on the queen bed, and a smaller collection on the floor in front of the bed, settled in, on and around a pair of fairly new, leather moccasins. The pile on the bed was still smoking.

"I think that's Bertram," Edna said, breaking into tears.

While Dunphee was staring at the ashes on the bed, he pulled a handkerchief out of his pocket and covered his nose. If that was Bertram, he thought, he'd lost a lot of weight or the fire that consumed him had gotten incredibly hot—so hot that it probably would've burned down the whole house. Dunphee glanced at the house shoes and then the shape of the ash piles. It looked like Bertram had probably burned to death, but to the point of cremation? It was a new one on Dunphee. He continued to scan the room for clues. When he turned back to Edna, she was still crying.

"Did Bertram smoke?" he ventured.

"No."

"If I didn't know any better," Dunphee continued, "I'd say someone poured gasoline on him and lit him on fire. That or jet fuel. But I don't see or smell any gasoline and jet fuel is tricky to handle. And if gasoline was poured on Bertram, what are the chances that someone could do that without spilling any. . . or cause him to burn up without burning anything else up?"

"So, you think it's him? I mean, there's hardly anything left."

Dunphee spotted something on the bed and took a ballpoint pen out of his shirt pocket. He stood next to the bed and picked at the ash pile that appeared to have been the head. He isolated a clump of cinder that contained a small, twisted bead of silver.

"Did Bertram have fillings?" Dunphee asked.

"I think so."

"This looks like part of a filling. And I assume those are Bertram's moccasins?"

"Yes."

"I guess this is Bertram. Is there anybody else it could be?"

"No."

Dunphee took her at her word, but there was still the job.

"Edna."

"Yes."

"I don't mean to be indelicate, but I have to ask. You didn't do this, did you?"

"No, Billy."

"I had to ask.

"I know."

Dunphee tried to lighten the moment. "Edna—this ain't some old cowpoke you hooked up with, and things went south?"

"Oh, goodness, no," she said, with a weak smile. "Since I lost Arthur, you know I never. I don't need another man to take care of."

"I hear you. I've felt the same way since Linda passed."

"Oh, I still can't believe it," Edna said. "She was so young."

"Yes, she was."

Dunphee nodded and Edna managed another weak smile.

"What happened to Bertram, Sheriff?"

"I'm not real sure."

They stood there, quietly, considering what Dunphee assumed were Bertam's remains. He dialed the office and requested a couple of deputies and a Crime Scene Investigation unit. He led Edna out of the room, shut the door and replaced the towel. Then, they went out into the yard to wait in fresher air.

When the deputies and the CSI unit arrived, Dunphee headed to Tyler. Old man Bertram's odd remains had ruined his appetite, but he knew he should eat something. He got to Nat's Dine-In just after 10:00 a.m. and had the place to himself. Not many late-risers frequented Nat's.

He took a chair in a wall booth that featured a crooked, eight-by-ten snapshot of Nat (a tall African American man and the long-time, sole owner and proprietor of the Dine -In) standing next to Earl Campbell, Tyler's most revered native son. Nat's hair was black and full in the picture, but of late it had faded white and was receding. Nat appeared and poured Dunphee a cup of coffee.

"What'll it be, Sheriff?"

"One egg over medium," Dunphee said, adding "one piece of bacon—make that two—and a side of grits."

Toast?"

"One piece of wheat toast."

"Coming right up, Sheriff."

Nat was close to Bertram's age, and also from Harkin, but he grew up in Kilgore. Dunphee had known him almost all his adult life.

Nat had served in the military and relocated to Tyler in the 1980s. He started the diner and made it into a local landmark, popular because it was folksy and Nat was the genuine article. When the occasional, uninitiated customer made or inquired about to-go orders, Nat was known to point at the sign out front and remind them he ran a *dine-in* establishment. If they wanted fast food, he'd add, they could take their business to the Whataburger down the street. Nat was black and—excepting Earl Campbell—black was underappreciated in Tyler. But Nat's Dine-In reminded folks middle-aged and older, black and white, of what things used to be like in East Texas before everyone bent their knee to the hurry up and plunked down in front of cable TV after the daily race.

Dunphee sipped on his coffee. He had to see his grandmother later and he didn't relish the thought of mentioning Bertram's passing. His grandmother and Bertram had known each other when they were young. She also knew Nat.

Nat appeared with Dunphee's breakfast momentarily. The bacon smelled good, perhaps especially after the olfactory trauma he'd experienced at Edna's.

"How things goin'?" Nat asked.

"Okay," Dunphee answered. "But it's early yet."

Dunphee finished his bacon.

"When you going to retire, Nat?"

"The day after never. How's yer grandmama doin?"

"She's alright. I'm going to see her at the home tonight."

"Please send my regards."

"I will. But I think she'd rather me bring her a piece of your pecan pie."

"Bring her by later. I'll have it made fresh."

Dunphee picked at his egg.

"How long you known my grandmother, Nat?"

"Since I was around six. She was older, I think eleven or twelve when we left."

"Did you know Tieg Bertram?"

Nat looked directly at Dunphee and then glanced out the front window. "Hmm. You could say that. I knew *of* him."

"I think my grandmother knew him."

"Probably so. It wasn't a big town back then."

"Still isn't."

"No. It isn't." Nat rolled up his sleeves. "Tieg Bertram left Harkin 'round same time my folks did, been gone since forever. Why you askin' about him?"

"I think he's dead. I just saw what I took to be his remains over at Edna Jenkins's place."

"Here?" Nat asked abruptly. "In Smith County?"

"Yep. I just found him in a pile of ashes."

Nat's face changed and he tried to conceal whatever he was thinking by staring at the egg left on Dunphee's plate.

"You okay, Nat?" Dunphee asked.

Nat continued to stare.

"That's sad to hear," Nat said, seeming dazed.

"Nat?"

"Yes, sir?"

"What's wrong?"

"Nothing, Sheriff. Nothing. There's just some water under that bridge. Bertram and some others caused some trouble for us back in the day."

"I never heard that."

"We don't talk about it. Nobody talks about it."

"Can you tell me about it?"

"Rather not, Sheriff."

Dunphee leaned back and stared at Nat, surprised. Nat stared back.

"It was a long time, ago, Bill Dunphee," Nat said pointedly. "I think we'd all be better off if we left it there."

Dunphee was shocked, but he didn't show it. Nat had always been oak solid, and here he was, rattled. Harkin wasn't big enough for secrets. Hell, neither was Tyler.

Nat noticed the crooked eight-by-ten of him standing next to Earl Campbell and straightened it.

"I gotta' get back to the kitchen," he said nonchalantly. "Anything else I can get you, Sheriff?"

"No, thanks."

"Thanks for coming by!"

"Thank you."

Dunphee set a ten-dollar bill under his coffee cup and left.

When he got into his patrol car, Dunphee turned on the ignition and sat for a moment. He was mildly stunned. *What just happened in there?*

Dunphee phoned the Department and told his secretary to hold his calls, except for those regarding the investigation into Tieg Bertram's death. He sat for several moments, thinking, and then turned off the car's ignition and went back inside. Nat was still in the kitchen.

Dunphee sat down in a wall booth closer to the kitchen and waited. After a few moments, Nat returned to bus Dunphee's dishes. He was carrying a dishrag and a plastic bus bin.

"We need to talk," Dunphee said.

"That right, Billy?" Nat replied coolly. "You askin' as a friend? Or you telling me in an official capacity?"

"You know me better than that."

"Do I? I know—*as a friend*—I just asked you to leave this alone."

"I'm aware. But I'm trying to find out what happened to Bertram."

"Doesn't matter."

"What does that mean?"

"Maybe he got what was comin' to him." Nat regretted the statement as soon as he made it.

Dunphee's eyes narrowed and he considered what Nat said carefully. He doubted Nat was involved in Bertram's death, but the way he initially responded to the news was peculiar.

"I see them wagon wheels spinnin' in your head," Nat continued. "Don't let this thing get stuck in yer craw. Won't do you no good. Won't do any of us any good." Nat started gathering Dunphee's dishes. "I know you got a job to do," Nat added, over his shoulder. "But this one—it's ancient history. Let the dead bury the dead."

Dunphee switched seats in the booth. He was now staring at Nat's back. "You have any idea how crazy you're sounding?"

"Yes, Billy. I do." Nat turned to head toward the kitchen with the dishes and then stopped at Dunphee's table. "I'm an old man, Billy. You oughta' let me alone. I slipped up. That's all."

"This just gets worse and worse," Dunphee groaned.

Nat laid the bus bin aside and sat back down across from Dunphee. He was quiet for a minute, thinking, staring into nothing. Finally, he spoke.

"Remember the 'slaughter rule?'" Nat said. "In little league baseball . . . when you were a kid?"

"Yes."

"This is like that, Billy. For a long time, white folks around here ran up the score, but there was no rule against it. There were no rules against killing black people. Or raping black women. And the game went on and on. White folks just kept on going, running up the score—and black folks just kept on dyin'. And suffering. It was before your time, most of it. But I'm gonna say this, and you need to hear me, Billy. We're friends and you need to really hear me."

Dunphee nodded.

"What happened to Bertram ain't got nothin' to do with anything goin' on today. It's a game that started a long time ago . . . and was bound to finish. Your grandmamma obviously didn't tell you about it . . . she had her reasons. I can't tell you about it now. It ain't my place.

"No one told you and no one told anyone, because they were scared or ashamed. And it's been like that here since Johnny Reb came limping home after the war. My family left Harkin 'cause of it. And our home town is still a nothing little smudge on the map 'cause of it."

"What are you saying?" Dunphee asked.

"I'm sayin' what happened to Bertram may have been a long time coming, probably because he stayed away."

"Stayed away. Stayed away from what?"

"What he did, Billy. *What he did.*"

Dunphee sat in the booth dumbfounded. He had no idea what Nat was talking about. And he suddenly felt like he had no idea where he was from or who the people he grew up with were. "Nat," he said. "I can't let this stand. I feel . . . I feel undermined."

"Sorry," Nat replied. "But that's a fine word for it. That's exactly how I might've put it."

"You know I gotta' know," Dunphee added.

Nat looked Dunphee directly in the eyes. They stared at each other for a long moment and then Nat nodded.

Nat told Dunphee he had to get ready for the lunch crowd, but that he would meet with him later. At the library, at 3:00 p.m. Dunphee hadn't been to a library in years and he regretted it. He decided to move up his date with his grandmother. As he got up to leave, a familiar face in a frame caught his eye. This image wasn't crooked. It was a newspaper clipping of Byron Payton.

Dunphee had seen it a thousand times. Payton's head was slightly cocked to the right and his hands were gloved. He was hugging a heavy bag, probably during or after a workout, and he was smiling.

Dunphee's grandmother's nursing home was not too shabby and had been her idea. He had protested, but Alta Jean, as his grandmother preferred to be called (by everyone except her grandson), usually got her way. When he entered her room, she was sitting on the side of her bed, staring out the window.

"Alta Jean," he said.

She turned her head slowly. "Hello."

"Hello. How are you?"

"I'm alright." What about you?"

"Doing okay."

"How are my great-grandbabies?"

"Still off at school, one at A & M and one at UT."

"That'll make for *uh* . . ." Alta Jean trailed off.

"An interesting Thanksgiving," Dunphee said, finishing her sentence. "Yes."

"Thanksgiving? *Already?*"

"No, Me-Maw. Not yet."

"Seemed awful soon."

"Yep. We've got awhile."

Dunphee looked around the room at all of Alta Jean's old pictures. The TV was on but the sound was turned down.

"I saw Nat," Dunphee added.

"How's he doing?"

"He's doing well. He sends his regards."

"Oh, I miss him. He's a sweet man."

"He's a good guy. Always was."

"Yes."

Dunphee walked over and sat in a chair next to Alta Jean's small couch. Then, he stared at her. She kept her white hair neat and her nails filed, but she was visibly frail. She tried to carry herself well, but her advancing age was really starting to show. Alta Jean noticed that he was staring.

"Can I talk to you about something?" Dunphee asked.

"I suppose . . . so."

"Okay. But you may have to put on your thinking cap."

"Okay. I can do that."

"Do you remember Tieg Bertram?"

Alta Jean glanced downward and was slow to answer. "Bertram. Yes. He moved away."

"Yes," Dunphee said. "What do you remember about him?"

"Oh. He was a bully."

"He was?"

"Yes."

Dunphee waited for her to elaborate, but she didn't.

"Yes," she repeated. "Why do you ask?"

"Well, he came back over the weekend."

"Back . . ." Alta Jean said. *Here?* She turned to face Dunphee. "Bertram is here?!"

"Yes."

"Is he okay?"

"No."

Alta Jean clasped her hands and brought them to her face, her knuckles just under her nose. She appeared to be praying, but Dunphee knew she wasn't. It wasn't her way. Or his.

Alta Jean's hands were clasped tightly and they started to shake. She unclasped them and placed them at her sides. She held them there for a moment and started to sob. Dunphee came over and placed his arm around her shoulders.

"Are you okay Alta Jean?"

"No, Billy," she said, between sniffs. "I'm very tired." Alta Jean wiped her eyes. "Sorry," she continued. "I'm just so tired."

"You need a nap?" Dunphee inquired, perplexed.

"I don't know. Just let me lie down. I'll be better in a minute."

Dunphee hugged his grandmother and then helped her lay back in the bed. She closed her eyes and he stood over her, wondering what the hell was going on. When she fell asleep, he left.

Dunphee walked out to his patrol car and put the department on the horn. The CSI unit had wrapped up and Bertram's presumed remains had been transferred to the Coroner's Office. There was no official word yet.

Dunphee was frustrated and it was still early.

Alta Jean had finished raising Dunphee after his parents were killed in a car wreck. A head-on collision in Seagoville, south of Dallas. Drunk driver.

Dunphee was eleven at the time, about to turn twelve. He spent the rest of his adolescence on his grandparents' farm, milking cows, driving tractors and hauling hay. He hunted and fished and canoed the Nueces and Sabine Rivers. And he played sports.

Dunphee's grandfather passed not long after he graduated high school. His name was Roscoe and he was from Valdosta, Georgia. He was a tall quiet man, patient and witty.

Dunphee had loved him and his grandmother dearly, and now Alta Jean was all he had left. His aunts and uncles still all lived close, but he didn't see much of them. Especially after he came back from Sam Houston State University and joined the Sheriff's Department.

They had all been there on the night he fought Payton, like he was Harkin's own Great White Hope. His grandparents had remained composed after he lost, Alta Jean giving him a tight, loving hug, and his grandfather winking at him and nodding, realizing how hard he had worked to even put things in the hands of the judges. There had been no doubt in Dunphee's mind who won, but at least he went the distance. His aunts and uncles raised redneck hell.

That Nigger cheated.

Goddam spear-chucker!

Dunphee knew Payton had heard them, because Payton had looked at him the way black people you know and like look at you when a racist antagonist interrupts the moment you've shared. And the black person knows the circumstances will force you to agree with the antagonist or hold your tongue, a betrayal either way. But the way things were and sometimes still are.

Dunphee had lowered his head then, soundly defeated. And ashamed.

Twenty years removed, Dunphee sat in his patrol car hoping Payton had understood that. That he had been ashamed.

The dead don't bury the dead, he thought. *The living do*. To make things easier. To make it easier to betray them.

To Dunphee's way of thinking, the best way to bury the dead was to live right by them, and he figured that's why Byron Payton had remained a friendly presence in his mind all these years. Like his parents, his granddad and, more recently, his wife. They weren't meant to be disposed of. They were supposed to stay with you, in memory and spirit, guides as much as reminders. And they still made Dunphee as much of who he was as anything else.

Nat's advice had done no good at all.

What happened to Bertram and whatever it was he may or may not have done to deserve it stuck in Dunphee's craw and vexed him something fierce.

The cryptic talk, the warnings; he knew Nat was being straight. But the missing pieces, which seemed to indict Bertram and the entire town of Harkin, disturbed and frustrated him.

Alta Jean slept fitfully.

She kept mumbling a name under her breath, inaudible at first, but finally plain.

"Petty," she moaned.

She was back at her parent's place, early in the Depression. Up in her bedroom.

Her parents were out front, watching a group of Harkin citizens leave on horseback. They were followed by a one-horse wagon. A black boy was lying unconscious on the worn planks on the bottom of the wagon. It was Petty. His lips were smashed and he was bleeding from his side and his head above one eye. His hands were tied behind his back.

Alta Jean moaned again, barely audible.

She had been forced to do something that day.

Not by the black boy lying in the wagon, but by her parents and their neighbors and their friends. By the community.

When they brought Alta Jean out and she saw Petty in the wagon, she thought he was dead. *There was so much blood.*

When her parents asked her to do what she did, she thought it wouldn't matter because Petty looked like he was already gone. And her parents had told her to do it. Told her that if she didn't do it, they could lose the farm. Told her that if she didn't do it, their neighbors might turn against them and run them off.

Did she realize they could lose everything? Did she realize they might have to move away to make a living?

Alta Jean had done what her parents asked. Alta Jean had done what she was told and they had kept the farm and their friends and stayed in Harkin.

From that day forward, however, there were unintended consequences. Alta Jean suddenly enjoyed small town celebrity, importance, and pity—as a victim.

It was all a lie. And Alta Jean resented the lie.

Petty had been her friend. Petty had taught her how to catch crawdads and trap fireflies in jars. And she was trying to teach Petty his letters.

Alta Jean remembered hearing her parents argue that night after they carried Petty away in the wagon.

It's our fault, what they done to that boy.

How could we have known?

She shoulda' known better.

We shoulda' known better.

Petty wuz just a boy, a good boy.

Don't matter a lick. You know what the talk woulda' been.

Alta Jean hadn't seen what happened. She was told later, by a neighbor's bragging son. It had turned her blood cold, and she didn't think it would ever thaw.

And it didn't for a long time.

What happened to Petty was never forgotten; it was just never spoken of. Alta Jean was not inclined to forget, but it was an ugly thing to bear. She busied herself with chores and schoolwork. It had a lot to do with why she was late to marry.

Alta Jean had plenty of callers, but they were all from the Harkin area. One by one, she politely turned them away. Her mother began to worry she would be an old maid. Her father wondered if she was simply doing it out of spite. Alta Jean didn't believe the cold in her would ever subside, but it did. Life went on.

She met Billy's grandfather and she grew to love him. Their courtship was prolonged, because she had grown comfortable in the cold. She may have felt she owed it to Petty. But Roscoe was persistent and when he proposed, she told him about it, tested him with the truth, the shame of it, her long sadness and her soul laid bare. And a curious thing happened.

Roscoe didn't comfort her or try to help her rationalize it. Roscoe understood.

There had been a similar incident, maybe even worse, outside Roscoe's hometown. He had some experience with the same kind of guilt and revulsion. He was afflicted with some of the same pain and doubt and sadness. They were both disfigured on the inside and she realized they could shelter one another. And they did. When Roscoe passed, Alta Jean had Billy. Her surviving sons and daughters had become little more than East Texas detritus, subject to the same ebbs and flows of the communal neuroses that had seized the citizenry of Harkin when she was young. But

Billy was different. Billy was like her and Roscoe, capable of empathy. Conscience. And he, too, was alienated by his own decency in the midst of dimwitted hayseeds and slack-souled buffoons. They were everywhere and all at once, the products of a dangerous mob mentality that seemed to thrive in the environs of red dirt and piney wood forest.

Idiots like Tieg Bertram and his kind had fed off frenzy and reveled in it. Men like Billy usually stood back, and away, and tried to keep some perspective.

In Alta Jean's dream, Petty was awake and being drug by a rope tied around his chest and arms. He hadn't been dead in the back of the wagon and this disturbed her.

Petty was being led to a tall tree stump by a dozen white men. He was crying and calling out to the ones he recognized, to the ones he had worked for or grew up around—but they all ignored him. Disassociation was necessary. It made what they were about to do easier.

"Petty," Alta Jean repeated weakly.

Her eyebrows furrowed and she began to turn.

Though distracted, Nat worked the lunchtime crowd with his typical, imperturbable contrarianism. And customers still managed to spill coffee, forget to tip the waitpersons and asininely inquire about catering or "to go" orders.

When the lunch traffic began to fritter out, Nat thought on Dunphee's line of inquiry while he bussed tables.

It had never occurred to him that the lynching of Petty Smith would ever come up again—especially in a conversation with a white man. White folks were great at forgetting history that presented them less than favorably and even better at portraying folks who viewed them unfavorably, well, unfavorably. It was a crippling one-two punch and Nat had heard it all.

Jim Crow was a long time ago.

Reverse discrimination is the real problem.

If you people will just quit belly-aching about race.

He marveled at the simplicity of white avoidance and almost admired the sheer and utter gall of it. It was as if white folk really believed that black folk were incapable of keeping track of what had been done to them. It had been less than a year since James Byrd, Jr., was beaten severely and then dragged to death behind a pick-up truck carrying three young white men, and the first reporting on the crime had focused on Byrd's past issues with alcoholism. And once white folks at large got their head around the actual facts concerning the murder, they acted like it was the first time anything like that had ever happened in Texas.

Nat shook his head and checked the time. It was 1:45 p.m.

Nat was also dumbfounded that Bertram had come back. Nat was a young man in the early 1950s when the last incident occurred, and it had happened the exact same way. Lester Grissem had returned home for a funeral and one funeral became two. Lester was cremated before cremation was even a thing. And they had all known damn well or at least suspected the truth of it then. But everyone had just gone on about their business. Black folks and white.

Could Bertram have forgotten?

Nat found that hard to believe, but Bertram was getting old. Maybe he had gotten old enough he didn't care. Maybe he thought something had changed.

Nat thought on what it had meant to his own family. They had had some hard years after, forced to start again in a new town. Grissem's death had absolved them all. But too little, too late.

Nat finished cleaning a section of tables and carried his bus bin to the kitchen. Then, he abruptly told the girl behind the register he was taking off for the rest of the day.

Nat decided to go to the library early. He had started participating in a local African American genealogical research group on the weekends. He'd quickly learned his way around the library and was well-familiar with the microfiche machine. He figured he'd go on down and locate some of the articles he wanted to show Dunphee.

Dunphee was in trouble.

Bertram's death was inexplicable, his mother's reaction to it was puzzling and Nat's insinuated secrets about them both were unsettling. And when Dunphee remembered the phrase that seemed to describe what happened to Bertram, he immediately wished he hadn't.

Spontaneous human combustion.

It was straight out of *Night Gallery* when he was a kid. Or maybe it was *Kolchak: The Nightstalker*.

Oh well, he thought. He was up for retirement soon. Maybe he could buy the old Troup Boxing Gym and start a boxing club.

When Dunphee arrived at the library, Nat was waiting for him. There was a short row of three microfiche machines in the back corner, and Nat had them all to himself. He had microfiche spools installed in all three.

Nat smiled, stood up and shook Dunphee's hand. "You ready for this?" he asked.

"I don't know," Dunphee answered. "It doesn't matter. I need to know."

"Okay," Nat said. "First, let me give you some background. Last week you were on the news for that memorial the city put in on the west side of the courthouse square. The one for the fallen law officers."

"'Fallen Heroes.' Yes. Fire department and law enforcement personnel who died in the line of duty."

"And the ceremony was moving," Nat said, "and the water fountain was pretty and you had a good turnout."

"Yes."

"Have you ever noticed how you don't see a lot of black folks down there? Except to report to the courthouse across the street?"

"Not a lot, but some."

"Probably only a few. Nice memorial dedication, right? The courthouse, the monuments? You like it down there?"

"It's alright, I guess."

"Only 'cause you don't know any better."

"Well, tell me then."

Nat nodded. "And the same thing is true of Harkin. But I ain't ready to talk about Harkin. Or Bertram. Tyler first. We'll take a look at Tyler, first."

"Okay."

"You sure?"

"Sure."

Nat sat down at the middle microfiche machine and had Dunphee sit at the one on his left. He gave him brief instructions on how to scroll the microfiche forward and back and how to focus in and enlarge. Then, he enlarged a story on a page that he had already pulled up for Dunphee. It was from the October 30, 1895 edition of the *Dallas Morning News*. The title read "Roasted to Death."

Nat had Billy glance at it and then lean over and examine the article pulled up on his machine. It was from the October 31, 1895 edition of *Wills Point Chronicle*. The title read "Burned at the Stake."

"Is this the same guy?" Dunphee said.

"Yep."

"He was burned at the stake?"

"Yep."

"Where?"

Nat nodded at the microfiche machines. "Take your time," he said.

Dunphee began reading.

He learned that in late October, 1895, a black man named Robert Henson Hillard had been the only suspect in the alleged sexual assault and murder of a young white woman. And the victim, the only eyewitness, was dead. But Hillard hadn't faced a judge or jury. Dunphee learned that one of his predecessors, Wig Slerrit, had discovered Hillard asleep in a cotton pen near Kilgore. On Slerrit's's way back to Tyler, a large white mob surrounded him and relieved him of his suspect. Then the mob finished Hillard's transport, planted a steel rail in the middle of the present-day memorial section of the public square and burned him alive in front of a crowd of thousands.

Dunphee learned that Hillard's lynching party had taken its time, starting, extinguishing and restarting the fire over and over—letting it rise a little higher and burn a little longer each time—so Hillard would cook as slowly and painfully as possible.

"Oh . . . *my* . . ." Dunphee sighed.

Dunphee also learned that halfway through the ghastly proceedings, Hillard had begun smashing his head back against the rail he was bound to, attempting to bash his own brains in to escape the prolonged, horrendous suffering. But his agony elicited hoots and snickers from his tormentors.

"Is this for real, Nat?" Dunphee asked.

"Real as you and me sitting here."

Dunphee finished.

"The same part of the square where we erected the Fallen Heroes Memorial?"

"Yep."

"Damn."

"Damn is right. Now look at the story on the last machine."

Dunphee moved to the last microfiche machine in the short row. It displayed an article from the May 26, 1912 edition of the *Dallas Morning News*. The title read "Negro Meets Death at Stake in Tyler." The African American victim was Dan Davis. Like Hillard, Davis was accused of attacking a white woman, denied a trial and due process and burned at the stake on the west side of the courthouse square in front of a mob of thousands. When the flames had begun to consume him, he begged his executioners to slit his throat, but they ignored his pleas.

Dunphee finished reading again. His gaze met Nat's momentarily, and then he averted his eyes. "You think you know a place," he said. "There are bad things, but you assume the good outweighs the bad. But this . . . How could folks not know about this?"

"Some do," Nat replied. "But not many. And they're almost all black and old-timers, like me. No one talks about it. People don't want to hear it."

Nat and Dunphee remained silent for a minute or two and then Nat sat down at the first machine and began rewinding the microfilm.

"Those are just the ones they burned in town," he continued. "They burned more out at Camp Ford during the Civil War. It was the largest, Confederate prisoner of war camp west of the Mississippi. They burned several black men there, black men enlisted in the Union army or Union sympathizers amongst the slave population."

Dunphee turned back to the machine he was sitting at and mimicked Nat. They rewound the rolls of microfilm and reinserted them in the small boxes they came from.

"Someone should do something," Dunphee said. "Is there anything we could do? Davis and Hillard ought to have memorials themselves."

"That's all well and good, sure. But if you ever suggest it you'll lose your job or they'll bury you under the damn thing if it's ever erected. This is just what went on. It started during the war and continued after Reconstruction. There was no slaughter rule. There were no rules at all where blacks were concerned. Remember those three boys that dragged 'ol James Byrd to death in Jasper, last year? That one that received the death penalty? He'll be the first white man that ever received a death sentence for killing a black man in Texas. Think about that."

Dunphee shrugged. It was a lot to take in. "What can we do?" he asked.

"Nothin," Nat replied. "But we know. You know—I know. We can know. And maybe later we can tell more people. Right now, no good'll come of it. People don't wanna' know and wouldn't believe you if you told 'em. Let's talk about Harkin."

11

Nat told Dunphee what he knew. The Tyler atrocities were a primer, but as bad as they were, they were tame compared to what happened in Harkin.

Pettigrew Smith, a thirteen-year-old black boy, had simply been accused of being sweet on Dunphee's grandmother, nothing more. Petty's mother had worked in the fields with and for Alta Jean's folks, and it was natural that Alta Jean and Petty started playing together, running the pastures and exploring the creeks. But the townsfolk took note and were not unfamiliar with how their neighbors in Tyler handled their "negro" problems.

The town of Harkin was the proud hometown of two Confederate war heroes, both deceased, and the youngest son of one was still insanely bitter about the "War of Northern Aggression" and Lincoln's attempt to turn Dixie into "Nigger York." This yokel, whose name escaped Nat, had been the instigator; seven Harkin boys, including Lester Grissem and Tieg Bertram had done the deed.

With the son of one of the dead Confederate heroes coaching, Petty was accused of making eyes at Alta Jean and beaten. Then, "making eyes" became "making advances." More young men beat on Petty and by the time he was brought unconscious before the town elders, his guilt was a foregone conclusion. All that was missing was a semblance of proof.

Petty was taken out to Alta Jean's home and she was coerced to give it. Then Grissem, Bertram, Tom Huff, Jack Walls, the son of the Confederate hero, and three others took Petty to a clearing heading out of town (toward New Summerfield), and bound him to a tall, broad tree stump with rope. Then they cut his tongue out, castrated him and bullwhipped him till he was unconscious.

The soaking, antiseptic sting of kerosene revived Petty, just in time for Tom Huff to apply the torch. Huff ridiculed him first, asking him if he had any last words. Blood poured from Petty's mouth and tears streamed down his cheeks. As the others laughed, Huff set Petty aflame.

"Even without his tongue, they say he wailed for several terrible minutes," Nat said. "Eventually the flames burned through the ropes holding Petty up. He fell over. And even after the fire had burned him chimney chute black, something inside held on. Right as Huff walked over to poke Petty's charred body with a stick, Petty suddenly writhed and contorted, twisting away from the coals."

"Oh, god," Dunphee said.

"It scared the hell out of the lynching party. Bertram supposedly yelped out loud and Huff threw up. The son of the Confederate hero dropped to his knees. But Jack Walls and one of the others started stomping on what was left of Petty and kicked him back into the fire. Huff gathered some more brush and struck Petty's head with a chunk of it, revealing his white skull plain through his charred scalp. And then they just piled the rest of the wood on top. When Petty had burned down to cinder, they left. And that's when things got really scary."

"When did my grandmother find out?" Dunphee asked.

"I'm not sure. Once her folks got wind of what happened, I think they kept her locked in for days."

Dunphee's phone rang and he answered it. He nodded a few times and said "yes" and "thanks" and hung up. Then he turned back to Nat.

"That was the lab," Dunphee said. "Those are Bertram's ashes."

12

Nat and Sheriff Dunphee left the library and went to the courthouse square. Dunphee gave Nat a ride and they parked on the west side. Then, Dunphee went over and stood in front of the Fallen Heroes Memorial. Nat joined him.

"It's a nice monument," Nat said.

"It is," Dunphee replied. "I certainly prefer it to the one dedicated to the Confederacy back towards the courthouse—but you didn't hear me say that out loud."

"I understand," Nat said. "I do."

Dunphee sat down on a park bench and Nat joined him. "It doesn't seem like a bad place, does it?" Dunphee asked.

"No," Nat replied. "It's not too bad. It's a lot better than it was."

Dunphee laughed out loud. "Sorry," he said.

"No," Nat said. "I understand. It's crazy. Sometimes I feel like we're still living without slaughter rules . . . Here at home and overseas. Other times, I think we've come a little way."

"So, what you told me so far wasn't scary?"

"It was scary, but not real scary. Not hide-under-your-bed, tooth-rattling-scary. White people had burned plenty of black boys at the stake in Texas before Petty."

"Shit."

"Yep." Nat looked around to make sure no one was within earshot. "The thing is, the next morning Petty's remains were gone."

"Yeah?"

"Yep. The tree stump was burned all to hell, but Petty's ashes were gone."

"Holy crap."

"It frightened the lynch party at first, but then they decided it was some kinda' prank or black folk just tending to their dead. Members of the small lynch-mob told some folks and later, after some time had passed and they were no longer afraid, they did some bragging. Word got around. Nothing was ever done about it. Petty's mom moved away. Dallas, I think."

Dunphee took off his hat and placed it on his knee.

"About a year later," Nat continued, "Tommy Huff disappeared. Got up early one morning to milk cows, and all they found was three or four piles of ashes under a cow. Sound familiar?

"Human remains?" Dunphee asked.

"They didn't have high technology in those days, Billy. Whadda' you think? They suspected, but they didn't know for sure. Didn't even singe the bone-dry hay around the ashes. But Huff was gone and no one ever heard from him again. Then, Jack Walls and two of the others disappeared the following week. All the same way—out in the dark, missing, a pile of ashes in one of the places they were supposed to have been. And that's when we had to leave."

"Leave?"

"Yep."

Dunphee chewed on it for a moment. "They couldn't explain what was happening," he deduced. "But they started to think they knew."

"Yep. A black boy had been burned at the stake and now white folks were disappearing."

"They thought someone in the black community might be responsible."

"Exactly," Nat said. "They thought we were retaliating somehow."

"Wow."

"Yep. But we weren't. We weren't stupid. In that day and age, angry white folks could run black folks out of entire cities, even counties. My family fled and so did the rest. Gave up our land and homes, whatever we couldn't carry. We started over.

"The son of the Confederate hero hung himself a few months later and the 'disappearances' seemed to stop. But what really happened—"

"*Bertram and Lester moved away*," Dunphee said.

"Bingo," Nat replied. "And you know most of the rest. Grissem came back for a visit in 1951 and got burned to a crisp. They called it a freak accident. I think any of the old-timers who'd convinced themselves that it'd been us behind the disappearances, finally considered otherwise. And, of course, Bertram stayed away almost for good."

"Was there anybody else involved? I mean—not that I'm buying a charbroiled Pettigrew Smith still walking around like some kind of vengeful ghost—but was there anybody else Petty could be targeting?

"No one else still alive was directly or even indirectly involved, Billy. Except maybe your grandmother."

"Oh, shit."

Dunphee dropped Nat off at the restaurant and headed back over to the nursing home. Alta Jean was waiting.

When he saw her, he hugged her as if he hadn't seen her in years.

"Take it easy, kiddo," she said, smiling.

"Just glad to see you, Mee-Maw."

"Glad to see you, too, Billy. But it's only been a few hours."

Billy smiled. She was feeling better.

Alta Jean turned off the silent TV and they sat in the chairs in front of it.

"It's a little before your time, Billy," Alta Jean said. "But do you remember those old cathedral-looking radios?"

"Maybe. I think so. I know I've seen pictures."

"We used to have one when I was younger. A Philco 90. It was a tired old thing It would lose the signals. You could set it on and leave it on your favorite channel, and then, when you turned it on again, the signal would be gone or it wouldn't be there all the way. We'd turn it off and when we turned it back on a few hours later, the channel would be working fine. Never could tell when the signal would be all there."

"You want one of those old radios, Alta Jean?" Dunphee asked.

"Oh, honey," Alta Jean replied, laughing. "*I am one of those old radios.*"

"Alta Jean."

"No, William Taggert Dunphee, I'm dead serious."

"Okay."

"I'm not always around—and I know that— I wasn't completely around earlier when you came by. But I'm here now."

Alta Jean took one of Dunphee's hands and squeezed it. He squeezed hers back.

"I'm glad," Dunphee said.

"Me, too. But I need you to do something for me."

"What?"

"I need you to take me somewhere."

"Sure. Let's go do something. You want to go out to eat? You want to see a movie?"

"No, no. Nothing like that. Thanks, though. For offering. You're such a good boy, and a strong man." Tears filled Alta Jean's eyes. "I'm so proud of you."

Dunphee's eyes welled up. "Thanks, Mee-Maw. You know how much I love you."

"You know how much I love you, too, boy." Alta Jean got up and hugged him. He hugged her tightly again, and she laughed. "I wish I would remember to say things like that more often."

Dunphee released her from his embrace. She walked over to her closet and took a light jacket off a hanger. "I need you to take me back to Harkin, Billy."

"What?" Dunphee said, standing up. "No, Alta Jean. Why?"

"You don't *know* why?"

"No, ma'am."

"I called Nat's Dine-In inquiring after you a little while ago. I guess you were on your way."

"Oh, Alta Jean."

"It's okay. I know you know. But I'm glad you know. I sure miss Nat. You forget my piece of pecan pie?"

"We can go there, right now. I'll buy you the whole pie so you can bring it back here. And we'll get some vanilla ice cream to go with it."

"Maybe later, Billy. Maybe later. Please take me back home to Harkin."

"Why Mee-Maw? *Why?*

"They did keep me locked up for a spell," Alta Jean said. "But eventually things went back closer to normal—except Petty was gone. My best friend. I didn't know everything that had happened until later. I hadn't even been aware of some of the boys disappearing, or what they said were disappearances. But there were rumors."

Alta Jean walked to the center of the room and continued.

"They said on the days those young men disappeared, there was a black boy playing, just off a clearing on the road to New Summerfield."

"There's no clearing there now, Alta Jean. It's thick woods. Through and through."

"I don't doubt you, but I have to try."

"Try? Try and do what?"

"I'd like to see him again, Billy. You don't know what it's like. All these years. What happened. I'd just like to see him one more time."

"I doubt he's out there if he ever was. And if he is out there, he may not be the same."

"Maybe not. But I can try. Tieg came back and he's gone. Petty is here. I know it."

"What if he's looking for you?"

"Then there's no sense in hiding. Please, Billy. I'm ready. I been ready. I'm old. I'm not even myself some days."

"But I don't want you to go. I don't want to lose you."

"You'll never lose me, Billy. You never lost your granddad. You never lost your parents. I see all of them in you . . . when the dial on the radio is working.

"I never lost your granddad. I never lost your mama or your daddy. And I never lost Petty. And now he's back. What would you give to see Linda again? Or Papa Roscoe? Or your mama and daddy?

"Please help me, Billy. *Please.*"

Dunphee took a deep breath as he approached Harkin. His place was located down a turn-off opposite of the old county road to New Summerfield, and he thought about just driving his grandmother there. But she wasn't having it.

Alta Jean was light and anxious. She talked about Dunphee's granddad and his parents. She talked about his baseball games. Dunphee wished she could stay like this, suddenly full of vigor and familiarity. But he knew she was right about that part. The channel would come and go. And eventually it would fade away.

They took the county road toward New Summerfield just as it was starting to get dark. Dunphee was having second thoughts about the whole crazy narrative and still wasn't sure they'd see anything—but that's when they did. If they hadn't been looking for him, they wouldn't have seen him at all. And he wished they hadn't.

Dunphee started to speed up, pretend like he didn't notice; but his grandmother grabbed his arm.

"There he is," she said.

The figure was off to Dunphee's left, right at the edge of the thick woods. It was a curious sight and Dunphee felt his stomach drop.

He slowed down, pulling over about thirty yards in front of it, on its side of the road. When Dunphee opened his car door, the smell stung his nostrils and he drew his gun. His grandmother was already out on her side of the car and spryly walking around it toward the figure.

It didn't seem to notice either of them until Alta Jean said its name. Then it stopped.

"Petty," Alta Jean repeated. "*Petty, it's me.*"

The apparition turned to Alta Jean and then stepped in her direction.

Dunphee screamed "Stop!" and ran toward the dark form.

The figure turned back to Dunphee and limped stiffly forward. Dunphee yelled stop, again, but it kept coming.

"Billy," Alta Jean said. "Please. *Please.*"

The dark figure approached Billy, its roasted hide cracking, its eyes bright red, and its ghastly smile offering a profound image of menace. Dunphee stopped, watched the figure disbelievingly, and then and took aim.

As Alta Jean approached, the creature stopped and stood stock still, approximately fifteen yards from Dunphee.

Dunphee stared at it, a blackened human ligament. Twisted, repulsive. He could hardly believe what he was seeing—but he couldn't look away. He held his aim steady.

"Stay back, Alta Jean," Dunphee said.

She stopped, but Petty turned toward her and took an awkward step. Dunphee began firing and emptied his clip.

The dark figure was rocked backwards and sideways, tripping and then stumbling, every bullet producing a flash of yellow-orange flame as it penetrated or passed through the creature's blackened form. But it never collapsed.

As Dunphee reached for his spare clip, it slowly steadied itself and began coming at him. Alta Jean began screaming.

"No, Petty, no! STOP, PETTY. *STOP!*"

The apparition froze in its tracks, its lidless eyes still aimed forward in the direction of Dunphee. Alta Jean stepped closer.

"No, Alta Jean," Dunphee cried.

But it was too late.

The creature turned its head slowly, almost mechanically. Its grotesque face and teeth were expressionless.

Alta Jean beamed.

Dunphee raised his gun again, but he couldn't fire. He screamed "Mee-Maw" but Alta Jean didn't hear. He aimed his gun, but his grandmother took another step toward the creature and extended her left arm. The creature turned its body slowly and stood awkwardly, raising its right.

Dunphee watched helplessly.

Alta Jean's fingertips touched the creature's charred knuckles and there was a brilliant flash of blue flame.

In the glowing light, Dunphee saw Petty, a young black boy, at the edge of the woods. He was dressed in well-worn britches with suspenders slung over his over-sized, yellowing, hand-me-down long-johns. And facing him stood a young Alta Jean in a light, cotton dress, with more life in her than he thought he had ever seen before. Both of them were bright and happy, and so young. And they were smiling.

Smiling.

Dunphee started to cry.

Then, Alta Jean and Petty were laughing and Dunphee was no longer there.

As Alta Jean and Petty turned to run, the blue glow flashed yellow and orange and became flame. And then *they* were no longer there.

Finally taking a breath, Dunphee wiped his eyes with the sleeve of his gun hand, and then re-holstered his weapon.

He walked over to where they had stood last and saw two separate sets of ashes. Two sets of ashes touching just above the mid-sections, as if they were holding hands.

Dunphee began crying again, but this time he didn't stop. He dropped to his knees and let everything out.

Dunphee sat next to the two sets of ashes for half an hour, crying like a child, for everything that had gone on and for everything that had gone wrong. Then, he drove home.

At the house, he parked the patrol car and went inside and changed. He came back out with two empty, five-gallon plastic buckets and a shovel. He drove back out to the spot where he'd left Alta Jean and Petty. He shoveled them into separate buckets, put them in his truck and then transported them to his house.

The next day he drove out to the old, overgrown Harkin cemetery in a sorrowful daze. He buried Petty and Alta Jean in two separate sections of his grandmother's reserved plot, next to his grandfather's.

As he finished tamping down the dirt with his boots, his eyes welled up again; but he wiped the tears away quickly. Then, he shook his head and smiled.

He couldn't help it.

Tieg Bertram's bizarre death was described as a possible "spontaneous human combustion."

Local and state media outlets had a field day with it, but Dunphee refused to comment. He even turned down a call from the *National Enquirer.*

Alta Jean's remaining children filed a "Missing Persons" report after she had been gone for a week. They wouldn't have known, but the nursing home called.

Dunphee's aunt and uncles pushed for the county to issue a death certificate after six months, and he stayed out of it. When the certificate was filed, they fought over what was left of Alta Jean's bank accounts, but it wasn't much. And they never concerned themselves with purchasing a headstone for their mother's presumably empty grave.

Dunphee eventually bought one that matched his grandfather's and placed it at his grandmother's plot himself. He had the initials "P. S." etched into the center of the back of Alta Jean's marker in four-inch letters and didn't think anyone would notice.

For a long time, no one did.

AUTHOR

E. R. Bills is an award-winning, best-selling author and freelance journalist. His fiction work includes *Pendulum Grim* (2020), *Nature Calls* (2023), and *The Amulet* (2023) and he was the co-creator and is the current executive editor of the annual *Road Kill: Texas Horror by Texas Writers*, the first anthology of Texas horror, featuring works from Joe. R. Lansdale, Stephen Graham Jones, Robert E. Howard, Katherine Anne Porter, O. Henry, David Bowles, etc. His horror fiction writing has been compared to that of Stephen King, Ray Bradbury, Richard Matheson, Theodore Sturgeon and others.

Bills' nonfiction works include *Texas Obscurities: Stories of the Peculiar, Exceptional and Nefarious* (2013), *The 1910 Slocum Massacre: An Act of Genocide in East Texas* (2014), *Texas Far and Wide: The Tornado with Eyes, Gettysburg's Last Casualty, the Celestial Skipping Stone & Other Tales* (2017), *Texas Oblivion: Mysterious Disappearances, Escapes and Cover-Ups* (2021) *100 Things to Do in Texas Before You Die* (2022) and the upcoming *Tell-Tale Texas: Investigations into Infamous History* (August 2023).

Bills has also written for the *Austin American-Statesman*, the *Fort Worth Star-Telegram*, *Texas Co-Op Power* magazine, *Fort Worth Magazine* and *Fort Worth Weekly*. He currently lives in North Texas with his wife, Stacie.

STARKWEATHER IMPRINTS

P.O. Box 10553
River Oaks, TX 76114

NATURE CALLS
SHERIFF
SHERIFF
E. R. BILLS
A NEW TESTAMENT OF TERROR

May 2023

the AMULET

E. R. Bills

June 2023

57718 31003